Annabelle
the Drawing
Fairy

Special thanks to Rachel Elliott

No part of this publication may be reproduced, stored in a
retrieval system, or transmitted in any form or by any means,
electronic, mechanical, photocopying, recording, or otherwise,
without written permission of the publisher. For information
regarding permission, write to Rainbow Magic Limited,
c/o HIT Entertainment, 830 South Greenville Avenue,
Allen, TX 75002–3320.

ISBN 978-0-545-70830-2

12 11 10 9 8 7 6 5 4 3 2 1   15 16 17 18 19 20/0

Printed in the U.S.A.   40

This edition first printing, March 2015

Annabelle
the Drawing
Fairy

by Daisy Meadows

SCHOLASTIC INC.

Jack Frost's
Ice Castle

Campsite

Walkers'
tent

Daffodil
Cottage

Market Square

Pottery Hall

Sunshine
Cake Shop

Polly Painterly's Workshop

I'm a wonderful painter—have you heard of me?
Behold my artistic ability!
With palette, brush, and paints in hand,
I'll be the most famous artist in all the land!

The Magical Crafts Fairies can't stop me!
I'll steal their magic, and then you'll see
That everyone, no matter what the cost,
Will want a painting done by Jack Frost!

Contents

Camp
Breakfast

"I think Rainspell Island is my favorite place in the whole world!" said Kirsty Tate, twirling on the spot.

Her best friend, Rachel Walker, jumped up and grabbed Kirsty's hands. They spun around in a circle until they both fell down on the grass, dizzy and happy. It was spring, and the campsite meadow was full of daisies and buttercups.

"The sun always shines on Rainspell Island," Rachel said, laughing.

Rainspell Island was the place where Rachel and Kirsty had first become friends—and where they began their adventures with the fairies! Now they were back again with their families for Crafts Week.

All week, the girls could take different classes in all sorts of arts and crafts, from painting to jewelry-making. On the final day, there was going to be an exhibition and competition with prizes! Everyone who had participated in Crafts Week could enter whatever they had made. Rachel and Kirsty couldn't wait!

"Breakfast!" called Mrs. Walker.

The girls raced back to the tent where

the Walkers were staying. Mr. and Mrs.
Walker sat outside the tent, cooking
eggs, sausages, and home fries on their
camp stove.

"It's a beautiful morning," said Mr.
Walker. "I bet your parents wish they
were camping, too, Kirsty."

Mr. and Mrs. Tate were staying in a
local bed and breakfast, but Kirsty and

Rachel had decided to have a sleepover in the tent so they wouldn't have to be separated.

"So, girls, which classes are you taking today?" asked Mrs. Walker.

It was the second day of Crafts Week, and there were lots of crafts that the girls wanted to try.

"We haven't decided yet," said Rachel, sitting down on a stool and holding out her plate for some breakfast. "What do you think, Kirsty?"

Kirsty smiled and

held out her own plate.

"There are so many to choose from, I can't make up my mind," she said.

Mr. and Mrs. Walker started to talk about an exhibition they wanted to see, and Kirsty leaned closer to her best friend.

"I wonder if we'll meet another fairy today," she whispered.

"I hope so," Rachel replied in a low voice. "There are still six magic objects to find, and we don't even know where to start looking!"

The day before, Kayla the Pottery Fairy had whisked them off to Fairyland for the grand opening of the fairies' own Magical Crafts Week. Kirsty and Rachel had met the seven Magical Crafts Fairies, who showed them the magic objects they used to make sure everyone had fun doing arts and crafts.

The girls quietly ate their breakfast, thinking about all the things that had happened in Fairyland the day before. While they were standing in a crowd of their fairy friends, King Oberon and Queen Titania had announced that they would be choosing the best crafts to decorate their Fairyland Palace. But at that moment, Jack Frost and his goblins had thrown paint-filled balloons into the crowd, splattering the fairies with bright green paint! While everyone was distracted, Jack Frost and the goblins had

stolen the magic objects from the
Magical Crafts Fairies.

"I'm so glad that we managed to find
Kayla's magic vase yesterday," said
Kirsty quietly. "But we have to find the
rest of the magic objects—otherwise arts
and crafts will be ruined in our world
and in Fairyland."

"Jack Frost doesn't care about that," said Rachel. "He just wants to be the best at everything. Oh, Kirsty, we have to stop him!"

Jack Frost had decided that he was the greatest artist ever, and he had stolen the magic objects to make sure that no one tried to be better than him. They were hidden somewhere in the human world, so Kirsty and Rachel had offered to help the Magical Crafts Fairies find them.

Kirsty squeezed Rachel's hand.

"We just have to keep an eye out for the magic objects," she said. "After all, Queen Titania always says that we should wait for the magic to come to us!"

Suddenly, each girl felt a hand on her shoulder. Mr. Walker leaned forward between them.

"What did you say about magic?" he asked, raising his eyebrows.

Kirsty and Rachel exchanged worried looks. How much had Mr. Walker heard?

Art in
the Garden

"I'm glad that you think Crafts Week is magical," said Mr. Walker with a grin.

Rachel and Kirsty let out sighs of relief. He didn't realize that they were talking about the fairies after all!

"We're planning to go to an exhibit this morning," he went on, handing them a Crafts Week brochure. "A local artist called Sara Sketchley is showing a collection of paintings at her house. Why don't you come with us? She's teaching a drawing class in her garden, and you could join in."

"That sounds like a fun thing to do on a sunny day," said Rachel.

Kirsty nodded in agreement, so the girls hurried into the tent to pack their bags with the right equipment. They picked out two sketchbooks and filled their pencil cases with colored pencils,

erasers, and pencil sharpeners. Then they helped Mr. and Mrs. Walker wash and dry the pans and plates from breakfast.

"Time to go," said Mrs. Walker, checking her watch. "The drawing class starts in ten minutes."

They zipped up their tent and headed across the meadow. Rachel and Kirsty raced each other to the gate, and then waited for Mr. and Mrs. Walker to catch up.

"We need to keep a lookout for goblins today," said Rachel. "I bet Jack Frost has ordered them to hide the fairies' magic objects carefully."

Mr. and Mrs. Walker joined them and led the way down the road to Sara Sketchley's house. It was a pretty little cottage with pink roses around the door

and honeysuckle trailing around the
windows. The front yard had been
turned into an outdoor gallery.
Paintings hung from the trees and were
propped up in the flowerbeds.
Everywhere the girls looked, they saw
beautiful art!

"These roses look so real," said Kirsty, gazing at a painting that dangled from an apple tree. "I feel like I could reach out and touch them."

"Sara Sketchley obviously draws things from her life," said Mrs. Walker, looking around at the flower-filled garden. "She must be an amazing gardener as well as a talented artist."

"Her whole house must be an art gallery," said Rachel.

She pointed to a sign painted on a piece of driftwood.

More paintings this way ➡

The arrow was pointing into the house.

"Should we go inside?" Mr. Walker suggested.

"Is it all right if Kirsty and I explore a little?" Rachel asked.

Sara Sketchley's garden was the size of a small park, and the girls were eager to look around.

"Of course," said Mrs. Walker. "We'll see you later."

Rachel and Kirsty found that the garden was full of wonderful secrets waiting to be discovered. They saw a clear stream gurgling across the garden,

over a water mill, and under an old stone bridge. They even spotted a sign pointing the way to a garden maze on the other side of the bridge.

"That sounds fantastic!" said Rachel, remembering the other magical maze on Rainspell Island where they had met Fern the Green Fairy.

"I love mazes," Kirsty said. "Should we check it out?"

Rachel was about to agree when she saw a group of kids following a young woman to a grassy spot next to the bridge.

"I think that must be the drawing class," she said. "We'll have to check out the maze later. Come on!"

They ran over to join the others, and took a seat on the grass close to the bridge. The young woman was standing next to an easel, and she smiled at them. She had bright green eyes and brown curls that flowed over her shoulders. Her long skirt was decorated with a chain belt, and her feet were bare except for a silver ankle bracelet.

"Welcome to my drawing class, everyone," she said in a warm, rich voice. "It's wonderful to see so many kids who are interested in drawing. I'm passionate about art, and I believe that doing arts and crafts makes people feel calm and happy. So let's get started!" She smiled. "Please take out your pencils and drawing pads. I'm going to show you how to draw a lifelike rose."

Kirsty opened her bag and put her hand inside. Then she let out a little cry of surprise.

"There's something inside my bag!" she whispered to Rachel. "I felt it fluttering against my hand."

Rachel just smiled.

"It wasn't some*thing*, it was some*one*," she said. "Look!"

She pointed, and when Kirsty looked
down she couldn't help grinning from ear
to ear. Annabelle the Drawing Fairy was
smiling at them over the edge of Kirsty's
bag!

An A-Maze-ing Artist

Annabelle wore a pretty pastel shirt and cropped jeans. Her blond hair was shining in the sunlight.

"Hello, Annabelle!" whispered Rachel in excitement. "What are you doing here?"

"I've come to ask you to help me find my magic pencil sharpener," Annabelle said in a sweet voice. "Without it, drawings everywhere will be ruined!"

"Of course we'll help," said Kirsty.

"Thank you!" said Annabelle, ducking down into the bag again.

"Look carefully at the roses growing all around you," Sara Sketchley instructed the class. "I'm going to draw one first, and then I'd like you to give it a try."

Sara picked up a pencil and turned to the paper clipped on her easel. As soon as she pressed the pencil against the paper, the point broke.

"*Oops,*" said Sara with a little laugh. "That happens sometimes!"

She picked up another pencil, but this

one snapped in half. Sara frowned and
picked up a third pencil.

"Start with delicate, light pencil
strokes," she said.

She drew a line on
the paper, but it
wasn't gentle or soft.
It was a thick, angry
slash that almost
ripped right through.
Sara gasped.

"I'm sorry,
everyone," she said.
"I don't know what's the matter with me
today!"

Kirsty and Rachel exchanged a secret
glance. They both knew that it must
have something to do with the missing
magic pencil sharpener!

"I'm going to go get a better pencil from inside," said Sara. "Please start drawing your own lifelike sketches while you wait."

Rachel and Kirsty felt sorry for Sara. Jack Frost was ruining her art class, and they had no idea how to stop him! Rachel picked up a pencil, then put it down again.

"I can't concentrate on drawing," she said. "Let's see how the others are doing."

She stood up and walked around the grassy area, looking at the pictures the other kids were drawing. When she had seen two or three, she waved Kirsty over.

"Come and see these," she said in a low voice.

Kirsty picked up her bag and followed

Rachel. The other kids were drawing roses—but their pictures were all terrible! The roses looked ugly, with huge thorns and withered petals.

"These look nothing like the real roses," said Kirsty. "They're all pretty bad."

"All except that one," said Rachel.

She nodded at a boy in green overalls and a beret who was drawing the nearby water mill. His picture was

really good! It was so realistic that the girls felt like they could almost hear the stream gurgling.

Annabelle peeked out of Kirsty's bag, and just then, the boy looked up from his sketchpad. Annabelle gasped, and Rachel grabbed Kirsty's hand. The boy had a long, green nose.

"He's a goblin!" said Kirsty, shocked.

"I'll bet that's why he's drawing so

well," said Annabelle. "He must have my magic pencil sharpener!"

The goblin glanced over at the girls, and his beady eyes spotted Annabelle right away. He jumped up and knocked his easel over as he darted toward the bridge.

"Catch him!" cried Annabelle. "We can't let him get away!"

Rachel and Kirsty ran after the goblin. He raced over the bridge and into the garden maze. The girls followed, their feet clattering on the little wooden bridge. But when they ran into the maze, the goblin was nowhere to be seen. High hedges surrounded them. The girls reached an intersection and stopped.

"Which way?" asked Kirsty, glancing left and right.

"Quick, Annabelle, can you change us into fairies?" Rachel asked. "If we fly above the hedges, we can spot the goblin!"

Annabelle fluttered out of the bag and waved her wand. Instantly, the girls felt a tingling in their shoulders, and wings

appeared as they shrank to fairy size.
The maze hedges seemed twenty times
bigger, but Annabelle, Rachel, and
Kirsty zoomed into the air and hovered
above them.

"I see him!" cried Annabelle. "He's
over there!"

"No, this way!" said Rachel, pointing
in the opposite direction.

Kirsty looked down and groaned.

"Oh, no! There are *four* goblins in the
maze!" she exclaimed.

Litterbugs

As the girls watched, the goblins all met
up at the far side of the maze. One of
them was tearing pages out of a
sketchbook. He crumpled them up and
tossed them at the other goblins, who
squawked with laughter and threw them
everywhere. Balls of paper piled up on
the ground—and even on top of the
hedges.

"How dare they?" Rachel burst out.

She zoomed down and hovered in front of the goblins, frowning.

"Stop!" she demanded. "You're wasting paper and you're making a huge mess in the maze."

"Oh, be quiet, silly fairy!" cried the goblin with the sketchpad. "Mind your own business."

"This *is* our business," said Kirsty, flying down to hover beside her best friend. "You're being litterbugs, and it's everyone's job to keep things clean."

A tall goblin

danced around with his fingers in his
ears.

"I can't hear you!" he squawked in a
singsong voice. "I can't hear you!"

Just then, Kirsty saw a small, plump
goblin throw something the size of a
pencil sharpener into the air. Could it be
Annabelle's magic object? She swooped
down quickly and caught it in her
outstretched hand.

"Is it my pencil sharpener?" asked
Annabelle hopefully, darting down to
join Kirsty.

"No," said Kirsty
with a sigh. She held
out her hand and
showed Annabelle
an ordinary pink
eraser.

"I don't think these goblins have the magic pencil sharpener," said Rachel. "They're just messing around and causing trouble."

"You're right," said Kirsty. "If they *did* have it, they'd be using its magic to draw beautiful pictures, like the first goblin we saw."

"We have to keep looking," said Rachel. "He's somewhere in this maze."

"Let's spread out," suggested Annabelle. "If we fly low over the hedges, we'll find him eventually."

The three fairies fluttered above the maze, peering down among the green hedges. It was hard to see, because the bright sunshine made some dark shadows. But finally, Rachel spotted another goblin in the very center of the maze. He was sitting on a stone in a rock garden, drawing a picture of a nearby garden gnome.

Rachel waved to Kirsty and Annabelle. "It's him!" she said as they darted over to her. "Look, he's drawing again—I think he must have the magic pencil sharpener."

"But where is it?" asked Kirsty.

"And how can we get it back from

him?" added Annabelle.

They all thought hard, and then Kirsty's eyes sparkled.

"I have an idea," she said. "But if this is going to work, Rachel and I will need to be human size again."

They all flew down and landed on the ground in the shadow of a hedge. Then Annabelle tapped the girls with her wand, and they were transformed into

humans again. Rachel looked at Kirsty
with an excited and hopeful smile.

"What's the plan?" she asked.

"I think we should try to get the goblin
to draw pictures of us," said Kirsty. "If
we can get close to him, we might have
a chance to grab Annabelle's magic
pencil sharpener."

Annabelle clapped her hands with glee,
and Rachel gave her best friend a smile.

"That's a really good idea, Kirsty," she
said. "Goblins are so
vain about their abilities,
we might be able to
distract him for long
enough to find the pencil
sharpener."

Annabelle flew into
Rachel's pocket and

scooted down out of sight. Then Rachel
and Kirsty linked arms and walked
around the corner, into the middle of the
maze.

"We found it!" said Rachel in a loud
voice. "The center of the maze. Oh,
look—someone else got here before us!"

The goblin glanced up and spotted them standing there.

"It's that wonderful artist we saw earlier," said Kirsty cheerfully, making sure the goblin could hear her. "Let's go see what he's drawing now."

They walked over to the goblin, who had almost finished his picture of the gnome. But he jumped up and stood in front of his easel, his arms folded across his chest.

"Go away!" he snapped. "I don't speak to friends of that pesky fairy."

"What do you mean?" said Rachel with a laugh. "How could we be friends with a fairy when there's no such thing?"

Kirsty laughed, too, and leaned forward to look at the drawing.

"You're a really good artist," she said. "That gnome looks so lifelike! I bet you can draw people really well, too."

The goblin gave a smug little smile.

"I'm the best artist you've ever met," he said. "I'm even better than that Sara Sketchley."

"Can you draw us?" Kirsty asked.

"Oh, that would be wonderful,"
Rachel exclaimed, clapping her hands.
"Please say yes!"

Living Drawings

The goblin artist puffed out his chest with pride. "I can draw anything!" he said. "Drawing you two will be a piece of cake."

He flipped his drawing pad to a new page and turned the easel so he was facing the girls. They posed arm in arm while the goblin's pencil flew across the paper. After just a few moments, the goblin signed his picture with a flourish and turned it around to show the girls.

Rachel and Kirsty gasped. They knew it was the magic of the pencil sharpener, but the picture was astonishingly good. It was almost like looking in a mirror!

"You must be a great artist," said Rachel. "I wish I could draw like that! Would you teach us how to draw?"

"We could practice by drawing you," Kirsty suggested. "You have such an . . . interesting face."

"I bet lots of artists want to paint you," Rachel added. "You're so rugged and . . . um . . . handsome."

The goblin strutted back and forth in front of them and then struck a pose,

standing with one foot up on a
big rock.

"Sure, draw me," he
said. "Try to capture my
good looks and
charm!"

Kirsty pulled out
a pencil and
secretly broke off the
point. Then she held
it up.

"Oh, no, my pencil's broken," she said.

Rachel quickly broke off the tip of her
pencil, too.

"Mine, too," she said with a groan.
"And I don't have a pencil sharpener."

"Neither do I," said Kirsty, digging
through her pencil case.

The goblin looked annoyed. He had

been so excited about having his picture drawn.

"Hurry up!" he snarled. "Get on with it."

"Do you have a pencil sharpener we could use?" Kirsty asked. "If we can't find one, we won't be able to draw you!"

The goblin gazed at them, and the girls felt their hearts pounding. Would their plan work? Had they fooled the goblin?

"Don't you have other pencils you can use?" asked the goblin.

Rachel and Kirsty exchanged glances.

He sounded very suspicious. And they couldn't lie—they had pencil cases full of other pencils! What could they say? The goblin took a step toward them, and his face crumpled into a sneer.

"I know you!" he cried. "I never forget a face! You *were* with that horrible fairy earlier."

He stuck out his tongue and then ran away from them as quickly as he could.

"Annabelle, we need some drawings of hedges—quickly!" cried Rachel. She had a plan!

Annabelle zoomed into the air and

flicked her wand. A life-size drawing of a hedge dropped down in front of the goblin. He turned the other way, and another hedge drawing dropped in front of him. He thought the hedges were real! Believing that his path was blocked, he let out a loud wail.

"I'm trapped!" he yelled. "Let me out! I don't like this maze anymore!"

"Give Annabelle's magic pencil sharpener back," called Kirsty from the center of the maze. "Then we'll let you out."

"No way!" the goblin shouted. "Jack Frost told me to keep it away from you pesky fairies!"

"Then you'll just have to stay in the maze," said Kirsty.

"I don't like it!" the goblin whined. "I'm hungry! I'm thirsty! I want to go to the bathroom!"

"All you have to do is give Annabelle's magic pencil sharpener back," said Rachel. "It doesn't belong to you."

High above them, Annabelle gave a cry of excitement.

"He's opening his pencil case!" she called out.

Vivid Imaginations

Peeking around the edge of the paper hedge, Rachel and Kirsty saw the goblin pull a shimmering silver pencil sharpener out of his pencil case. He squinted angrily up at Annabelle.

"Here, come and take it," he said, annoyed. "But I hope it doesn't work for you! You rotten fairies ruin everything."

Annabelle fluttered down and took the
pencil sharpener from the goblin's bony
hand. It immediately shrank to
fairy size, and the magic
hedge drawings vanished in
a puff of fairy glitter.
Rachel and Kirsty
hugged each other in
delight, and
Annabelle gave a little
twirl in midair.

   The goblin shuffled back
to the picture of the gnome
that he had been drawing.
He picked up his pencil and
tried to finish, but his lines were all
squiggly. The gnome in his picture
started to look skinny and bony!

   The other goblins appeared from inside

the maze, and walked up behind him.
They didn't notice Kirsty and Rachel
standing off to the side.

"That's a terrible picture," said one of
the goblins scornfully.

"What do you know about drawing?"
snorted the goblin artist.

"Much more than you, judging by your drawing," snickered another goblin.

"Why are all the pages back in my sketchbook?" asked a third goblin, looking confused. "I crumpled half of them up, and now they're all as good as new."

"That's because littering is wrong," said Rachel, stepping out of the shadows. "You goblins need to learn to take care of the world around you. When Annabelle got her magic pencil sharpener back, she used her magic to clean up the big mess you made."

The other goblins ignored Rachel and spun around to glare at the goblin artist, instead.

"You fool!" the tall goblin shrieked. "How could you let that fairy get her magic object back? Jack Frost is going to be so angry with us again!"

"I was STUCK!" the goblin artist
screeched in anger.

"We need a plan," said the plumper
goblin. "What are we going to tell
Jack Frost?"

The goblins all sat down on stones in the rock garden and began to think hard.

Rachel and Kirsty couldn't help giggling at the goblins as Annabelle flew over to them.

"Follow me, and I'll lead you through the maze to the exit," she said.

Rachel and Kirsty left the goblins, who were still arguing about how to tell Jack Frost the terrible news. The girls kept their eyes on Annabelle, and she guided them all the way to the exit. There, she fluttered down beside them, with her magic pencil sharpener clutched in her hand.

"I'm not letting this out of my sight," she said with a big smile. "Girls, you've saved drawings all over the world. Thank you so much for helping me! Without you, I'm sure Jack Frost's goblins would still have my magic pencil sharpener."

"We were happy to help," said Rachel.

"Hopefully, we can do the same with the other missing objects," Kirsty added.

"I'll tell the other Magical Crafts Fairies how wonderful you are," said Annabelle. "Good-bye, and thanks again!"

As the girls raised their hands to wave good-bye, Annabelle disappeared in a shower of fairy sparkles.

"Come on," said Kirsty. "Let's get back to the drawing class."

Hand in hand, the girls ran across the bridge to the main part of the garden. Sara Sketchley was standing in front of the group of kids, holding up a finished picture of a beautiful rose.

"Now that you've seen me draw, I want to see what you can do," she was saying. "I'd like you to draw the most beautiful thing you can think of. It can be a person or a place, real or fantasy. Just have fun!"

Rachel and Kirsty exchanged happy smiles as they rejoined the class. They knew exactly what they were going to draw! They both took out their pencils and sketchbooks.

"My pencil is as good as new!" whispered Rachel. "Look!"

"Mine, too," said Kirsty, pressing her finger to the sharp point of her pencil. "Thank you, Annabelle!"

The girls were both concentrating on their drawings when they heard a familiar voice.

"Everyone seems to be hard at work here!"

The girls looked up and saw Artemis Johnson, the organizer of Crafts Week. She was walking toward Sara Sketchley, with Mr. and Mrs. Walker at her side.

"Hello, Artie," said Sara with a smile. "Yes, everyone's very busy. Let's take a look at how you're all doing."

She led Artie and Mr. and Mrs. Walker around the little group. When they

reached Rachel and Kirsty, Sara put a
hand on each of their shoulders.

"These are very interesting," she said.
"You girls are so talented! Kirsty's
picture of a magic fairyland is so realistic
that I can imagine being there! And,
Rachel, your fairy is so lifelike that it
looks like she could flutter off of the
paper and cast a spell!"

"What vivid imaginations," said Artie. "I can't wait for the exhibition at the end of the week!"

Mr. and Mrs. Walker beamed with pride. Kirsty and Rachel reached out their hands and linked their pinkie fingers in their secret sign of friendship. Kirsty had drawn the Fairyland Palace, which she had visited many times. Rachel had drawn a picture of Annabelle. They didn't have to imagine at all. They were drawing from real life!

As the grown-ups moved away, the girls whispered to each other about their very magical morning.

"Do you think we'll have another adventure tomorrow?" asked Kirsty.

Rachel looked at her best friend and smiled happily. "I'm sure we will!" she said.

THE MAGICAL CRAFTS FAIRIES

Rachel and Kirsty have found Kayla's
and Annabelle's missing magic objects.
Now it's time for them to help

Zadie
the Sewing Fairy!

Join their next adventure
in this special sneak peek. . . .

All Thumbs

"It looks like another magical morning, Kirsty," Rachel Walker said, gazing out the window of Daffodil Cottage. Even though it was still early, the sun was already shining. Rainspell Island looked green and beautiful with the morning light glimmering on the sea.

"Are you talking about the weather or our adventures with the Magical Crafts Fairies?" Kirsty Tate asked, her eyes twinkling. They'd arrived on Rainspell Island two days earlier and the girls were spending every other night in Kirsty's little attic bedroom at the b and b with the Tates, and alternate nights with Rachel's parents at a nearby campsite. The girls loved going to Rainspell Island for vacation because it was where they'd first met and become friends with the fairies.

"Both!" Rachel replied. Then she sighed. "Wasn't it mean of Jack Frost to steal the Magical Craft Fairies' objects?"

Kirsty nodded. "It was terrible," she agreed, "especially with Crafts Week here on Rainspell *and* Magical Crafts

Week happening at the same time in Fairyland. No one will have fun doing arts and crafts if Jack Frost has his way!"

While eagerly checking out the Crafts Week activities a few days before, Rachel and Kirsty had been thrilled to meet Kayla the Pottery Fairy, one of the seven Magical Crafts Fairies. Kayla had invited them to Fairyland to see King Oberon and Queen Titania announce the opening of Magical Crafts Week. The best and most beautiful crafts produced by the fairies would decorate the Fairyland Palace! Everyone, including the girls, had been very excited.

But the opening ceremony had turned into a disaster when Jack Frost and his goblins showed up, tossing balloons filled with bright green paint at the crowd. Queen Titania, Kayla, and the other Magical Crafts Fairies had been splattered with paint! In all the confusion, Jack Frost and the goblins had stolen the Magical Crafts Fairies' special objects.

Jack Frost had declared that he was the best at every kind of craft, and that no one else was allowed to be better than him. Then, with a wave of his ice wand, he and his goblins had disappeared to the human world — taking the magic objects with them. Rachel and Kirsty knew that the Crafts Week on Rainspell Island and in Fairyland would be a complete disaster while the fairies' magic items were missing. They'd immediately offered to help the Magical Crafts Fairies find the goblins and get their magic back!

"The pottery and drawing classes were so much fun," Kirsty remarked as she buttoned her favorite pink shirt. "But only because we found Kayla's magic vase and Annabelle's magic pencil sharpener just in time."

"And we'll do our best to find the other magic objects, too," Rachel said firmly. "We can't let Jack Frost ruin the whole week!"

RAINBOW magic™

Which Magical Fairies Have You Met?

- ❏ The Rainbow Fairies
- ❏ The Weather Fairies
- ❏ The Jewel Fairies
- ❏ The Pet Fairies
- ❏ The Dance Fairies
- ❏ The Music Fairies
- ❏ The Sports Fairies
- ❏ The Party Fairies
- ❏ The Ocean Fairies
- ❏ The Night Fairies
- ❏ The Magical Animal Fairies
- ❏ The Princess Fairies
- ❏ The Superstar Fairies
- ❏ The Fashion Fairies
- ❏ The Sugar & Spice Fairies
- ❏ The Earth Fairies

■ SCHOLASTIC

Find all of your favorite fairy friends at
scholastic.com/rainbowmagic

HiT entertainment

RMFAIRY10